ELEPHANT & FRIENDS

by Berniece Freschet   illustrated by Glen Rounds

Charles Scribner's Sons • New York

Text copyright © 1977 Berniece Freschet
Illustrations copyright © 1977 Glen Rounds

Library of Congress Cataloging in Publication Data
Freschet, Berniece.
Elephant and friends.
SUMMARY: Elephant's friends join together to help
repay his wisdom and kindness.
[1. Elephants—Fiction. 2. Friendship—Fiction]
I. Rounds, Glen, 1906-   II. Title.
PZ7.F88968El   [E]   77-13868
ISBN 0-684-15530-3

1 3 5 7 9 11 13 15 17 19 MD/C 20 18 16 14 12 10 8 6 4 2

Printed in the United States of America

To Gina
with special love

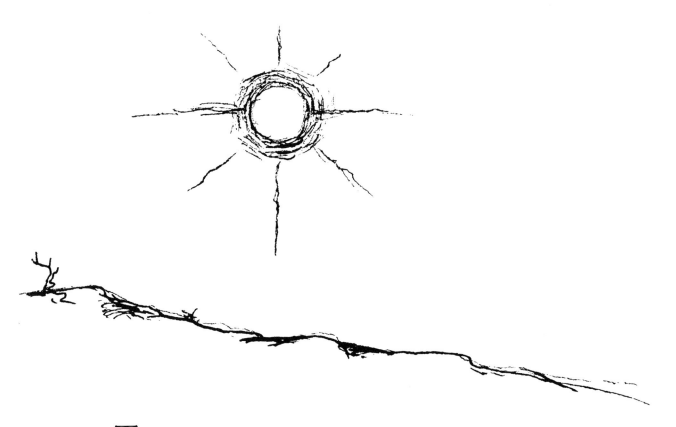

The hot sun shone down.

Heat waves shimmered in the air as Elephant walked slowly down the dusty path.

GAL-LUMPH! GAL-LUMPH! GAL-LUMPH!

Not long ago when Elephant walked by, trees shook and the earth rumbled. But today there was only a small quiver of the ground.

4

Elephant was not the powerful animal he used to be. Now
his wrinkled skin looked as though he were wearing a coat six
sizes too big for him.

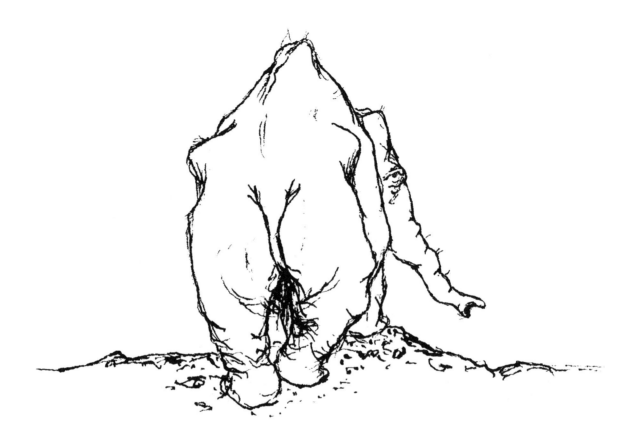

Elephant was tired—and very hungry.

This morning he had found only a mouthful of food. He looked for something to eat, first on one side of the path, and then the other. But the ground was bare. Not a small bush, not even a blade of grass was to be found.

The earth was dry and cracked.

It had not rained for many weeks.

A drought was on the land. Before long there would be nothing left to eat at all.

7

"Something must be done," said Elephant. "Something must be done soon or my friends and I will starve."

8

"What . . . what's that you say?" chattered a voice above. It was Monkey, sitting on a tree branch.

"He said that something must be done before all the food is gone," shrieked Parrot.

"I know," cried Monkey. "I haven't had a juicy mango to eat in so long that I've forgotten what one tastes like—but what can we do?"

"Yes," said Parrot. "What can we do?"

"We can find a new home where there is food and water for all," said Elephant.

"Good idea, Elephant. You are always so wise," said Monkey.

"But where can we go?" asked Parrot.

For a moment Elephant was silent, thinking. "We'll cross the desert and go live in the forest on the other side."

11

"That is a long way," said Parrot. "And even if we could cross the desert, how do you know there will be food and water there?"

"Long ago I lived there with my family," said Elephant. "I remember a wide river and leafy trees, and much food. It was very beautiful."

"Were there mangoes to eat?" asked Monkey.

Elephant nodded. "More than you could eat in a lifetime."

Monkey's eyes grew round. "If there was a river and many trees and more mangoes than you could eat in a lifetime, why did you leave?"

"One day hunters came," sighed Elephant. "Their guns filled the air with thunder. We were afraid and we ran. Some of us crossed the desert and came here to live."

"But what if the hunters come again?" asked Parrot.

"We'll have to take that chance," said Elephant. "I'd rather face an enemy I can see than stay here just waiting to starve."

"You are right, as always," said Monkey.

"Go and tell the others," said Elephant. "Have everyone gather any food and water they can find and we'll meet at the edge of the desert."

Monkey and Parrot hurried off.

Elephant walked on down the path. He came to Leopard, gazing sadly into a small pool of water.

"Look at our water hole," cried Leopard. "Just look at how it's dried up. Once I could see my whole face. Now all I can see is part of my nose and one side of my whiskers."

16

Leopard proudly stroked his whiskers as he gazed at his
reflection. "How handsome I was then," he sighed. "Oh well,
it's probably just as well that I can't see myself, since I'm only
half the leopard I once was." And he chuckled.

"It takes courage to joke at such a serious time," said Elephant.

"A laugh is better than a cry, I always say," said Leopard. "But I do wish my stomach would quit growling for food. Isn't there something we can do?"

"Yes," said Elephant. And he told Leopard of his plan. Then and there Leopard decided to join Elephant. And later, when they met Ostrich and Giraffe, they also decided to go along.

19

At the edge of the desert, Monkey and Parrot waited for
Elephant. "We've gathered all who want to come with us," said
Parrot. "But many were afraid to make the long trip."

"I am sorry," said Elephant. "But the sooner we leave, the
better for all. Is everyone ready?"

After each of the animals had called out "READY,"
Elephant raised his trunk and gave a mighty trumpet!
The long march across the desert began—Elephant leading
and a bedraggled-looking little group following along behind.

The sun climbed high in the sky.
Soon the air was heavy with heat.
It was Monkey who first stumbled and fell.

It was difficult for her to walk over the hot sand, especially as she was used to swinging from tree to tree. "I cannot go on," said Monkey. "You must go without me."

"No," said Elephant. "I will carry you." And he swung Monkey high onto his back.

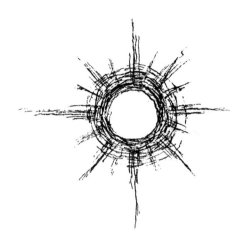

At the end of the second day the food and water was gone. The little group moved slower. Elephant kept up their spirits, telling them of the beautiful place that waited across the desert —

the wide flowing river,
the orchids and bright flowers that grew there,
and all the sweet fruits and juicy berries to eat.

"I can taste those mangoes now," said Monkey, licking her dry lips.

"I have to stop and rest," said Parrot. "My wings are so
tired that I can't flap one more flap."

"We must not stop," said Elephant. "Come and rest on my
trunk."

25

The animals struggled on.

"Just look at my poor feet," cried Ostrich. "Look at these blisters! I cannot walk another step."

26

"There's lots of room on my back." And Elephant raised
Ostrich high.

Next it was Gazelle and Hyena who fell. Soon there was no
room left on Elephant's back. He walked slower and slower.

It was the middle of the fourth day, when ahead, on the horizon, a wall of green shimmered through waves of heat. "What is it?" they all asked.

"The forest!" cried Elephant. "By the end of this day we'll be swimming in the cool river."

"Hurrah! Hurrah!" shouted the animals.

With new hope and strength they moved ahead. But they
had not gone far when, suddenly, Elephant's legs gave out. He
fell to his knees. He tried to get up... but he could not.

"We rested while you carried us," said Monkey. "Now we can walk the rest of the way." The animals slid down from Elephant's back. Parrot flew above.

30

Elephant tried again. But his strength was gone. He could
not get to his feet.

"Let's all boost Elephant up," said Leopard.

"Everyone together— *HEAVE!*"

31

The animals pushed and pulled.

They shoved and shouldered.

But it was no use—they were too weak. They could not budge Elephant. "I just need to rest a bit," said Elephant.

Parrot flew down. "Leopard...Leopard!" he shrieked. "Men with guns are coming this way! What shall we do? *What shall we do?*"

"They must be the hunters that Elephant told us about," said Leopard.

The animals were afraid. They wanted to run.

But Leopard said, "We cannot run away. If we do they will surely find Elephant. I have an idea. If you all do exactly as I say, I think we can still save ourselves. Parrot, fly above and keep watch on the hunters. Warn us when they get close.

"Now everyone—you smaller ones sit on Elephant's back.
The rest cover him with your bodies. When I holler *NOW!*—
Elephant, you rise up. Then everyone make the loudest noise
that you have ever made in all your lives."

Parrot flew down. "The hunters will be here soon," he shrieked. The animals hurried to their places.

"But Leopard, what if I can't get up?" said Elephant.

"You *must* get up," said Leopard. "It's our only hope."

35

Parrot shrieked a warning. "They're here! They're here!"
He flew down and perched on Elephant's trunk, spreading his
wings.

The hunters were upon them!

THEY RAISED THEIR GUNS.

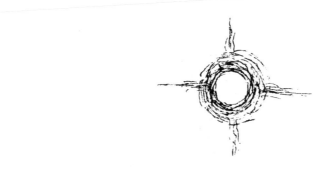

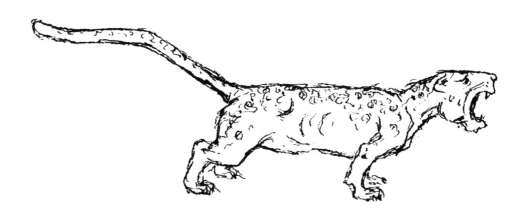

"Now!" cried Leopard. *"NOW!"*

Elephant heaved!

He shook!

He strained!

Summoning every last bit of strength, and with a mighty trumpet, Elephant lurched to his feet.

The animals began to shriek. The air vibrated with the noise.
Growling and roaring. Screeching and chattering.

39

Such barking and bellowing and hissing and clamoring—it was the most terrible sight and sound that had ever been heard or seen in all the land.

The hunters fell to their knees.
"A MONSTER!" they cried.
"A GIGANTIC TERRIBLE MONSTER!"
"Run for your lives. *RUN!*"

41

The men dropped their guns and ran. Along the way they told everyone they met of the huge, terrible-looking monster who was striped and spotted—

and furred and feathered,
and had wings and horns and *fifty* heads.

Everyone was so afraid that for a hundred years no one ever dared to come to that part of the land.

When the animals reached the forest, it was just as
Elephant had promised—

the wide, flowing river,
orchids and bright flowers growing everywhere,
and all the sweet fruits and juicy berries they could eat.

45

Each day the animals grew bigger and stronger.

Elephant became even greater and more powerful than he had been before.

GAL-LUMPH! GAL-LUMPH! GAL-LUMPH!

Now when he walked by, once again trees shook and the earth rumbled.

Leopard gazed at his reflection in the water.

"Look how handsome I am," he said, proudly stroking his whiskers. "Why, I'm twice the Leopard I once was." And he chuckled.

And for the next one hundred years,
all the creatures in the beautiful forest
lived together in peace and
great contentment.